Collins is an imprint of HarperCollins Publishers.

Jack & Jill
The Miracle Dog with a Happy Tail to Tell
Text copyright © 2009 by Jill Rappaport
Illustrations copyright © 2009 by Linda Solomon
Photograph of Jill Rappaport on page 11 courtesy of Heidi Gutman/NBC News

Manufactured in China.
Library of Congress Cataloging-in-Publication Data is available.
ISBN 978-0-06-173136-5 (trade bdg.)

Typography by Rachel Zegar
1 2 3 4 5 6 7 8 9 10
❖

First Edition

JACK & JILL

The Miracle Dog with a Happy Tail to Tell

by Jill Rappaport

with full-color photographs by Linda Solomon

Collins

An Imprint of HarperCollinsPublishers

For my beloved rescued brothers and sisters

Sweet Pea

Buckaroo

CJ

Petey

and Aunt Sassie and my cousins, Chance and Ozzie

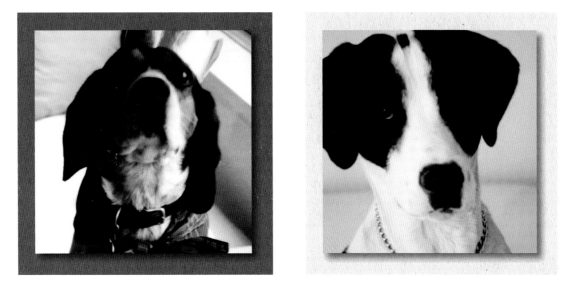

And in loving memory of Hampton & Shiner, who taught me
the ropes as a pup and watched over me into midlife

—Jack

Once upon a time, when I was just a puppy—only a few weeks old, and much too little to be out on my own—I found myself on a very scary street. I was hungry and tired and all alone. But then something very lucky happened. I wound up at just the right doorstep. There I met the special person who would become my mom for life.

I'm Jack.

She's Jill.

This is our story.

When my mom first named me Jack, I thought, Okay—it's short and cute like me! I'm a small German shepherd with a very sweet disposition. I'm a little bit afraid of a lot of things, not what you would expect from my breed. But what I lack in courage I make up for in heart.

Meeting my mom, Jill, was the greatest day of my life. Better than a new bone! She picked me up all scruffy and dirty and kissed me all over my face. I remember thinking, What is she doing? I just knew she was someone with a big smile, a warm lap, and a bowl of the best food I'd ever tasted. Jill was the first one to show me love and kindness—and I wasn't even housebroken!

I thought it was going to be just the two of us, but boy, was I wrong. *Woof! Woof!* Two big, scary, and extremely *loud* dogs came thundering at me. Hampton and Shiner were already part of my mom's family. At first I was nervous that they wouldn't like me, but once they sniffed me over and saw I was a good pup, they became my big brothers (as long as I didn't mess with Shiner's tennis ball or try to cut in on Hampton's snuggle time with Mom). And soon I was part of the family, too.

Life was grand, all right. I had hit the doggy lottery. There was always someone to play with and lots of mischief to be made and furniture to chew. (Of course, Mom didn't like *that* very much!) One day I even figured out how to open the front door with my paws, and my brothers and I snuck out. When Mom caught us, she tried to act stern, but she never could stay mad at any of us.

I was spoiled, but I wasn't the baby of the family for long. Soon Mom brought home Sweet Pea and Buckaroo, then a yappy little dog named CJ (man, she gave me a headache!), and finally Petey. Wow! Petey had the biggest head I'd ever seen—but he was very sweet and gentle. Now *I* got to be the big brother, and I took care of them the way Hampton and Shiner had taken care of me.

Just when I thought it couldn't get any better, Mom bought a farm! Now I had horses to play with, and deer to chase, and holes to dig, and fields to run through, and more deer to chase, and more holes to dig, and sticks to chew. . . .

Then one day my front leg started to hurt, and it was kind of hard to walk. My mom figured I had just been chasing too many deer and tried to get me to rest. But resting didn't help. Neither did the medicine she gave me. My leg still hurt a lot, and I was limping. After a few weeks, we both knew something was really wrong. My mom took me to the vet.

It turned out that I had a disease called bone cancer. The vet told us that when dogs get cancer, it's a lot like when people get cancer. I was very sick, but the same kinds of medicine and treatments that help sick people could help me.

Then he said that I needed an operation to save my life.

I was really scared. So was my mom.

The day of the surgery, my mom kissed me on my face, just like always, and promised to be there when I woke up. The doctor had to remove my hurt leg. I really didn't want to be a dog with only three legs—what if I couldn't run and play and have fun anymore?—but I really *did* want to get better, and this was the only way.

My mom was right there the minute I woke up. The operation was a success! The cancer was gone. CJ watched over me while I recovered at home. I still needed to have chemotherapy to make sure the cancer didn't come back, but Mom and I were very relieved and I was on the road to being healthy and pain-free again. Yay!

At first it felt really funny having only one front paw. To make it easier, my mom made sure I got lots of extra treats and kisses for being such a trooper. I had to learn to walk all over again. Actually, it's more like hopping, but it got easier the more I practiced.

I also learned that three-legged dogs have their own nickname: tripods. And I wasn't the only one! Tripods are all over the place! Lots of dogs have had cancer like I did or have been in accidents where they lost a leg. We tripods have our own websites, T-shirts, songs—and lots of books written about us. People even call us "miracle dogs."

I don't feel like a miracle. I just feel like a regular dog who was very lucky. Everything is back to normal. I still hang out with Buckaroo, Sweet Pea, CJ, and Petey. When we play together, they're a little more careful with me. And yes, that yappy little CJ still gives me a headache. (But I love her anyway!)

I don't look like most other dogs, but everyone loves me just the same. I may not do things the same *way* other dogs do, but I know I can do the same *things* they do—just a little slower.

There's no place I'd rather be than on our farm with my family. Now that I only have three legs, do you know what I love to do best?

Play with the horses, chase deer, dig holes, run through the fields, chase some more deer, dig more holes, chew sticks. . . .

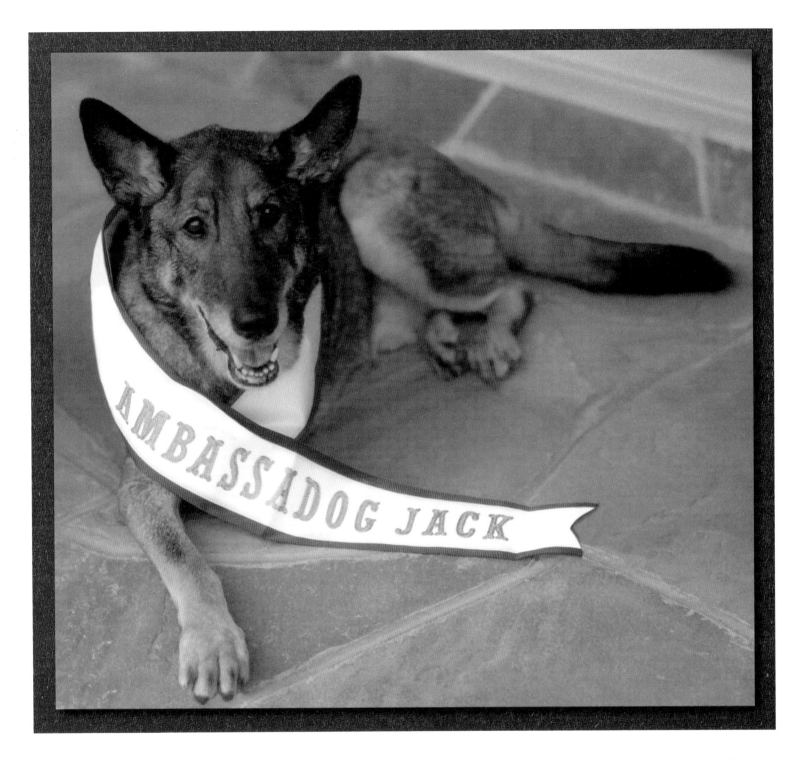

Life is still grand, all right. In fact, I've even become somewhat of a celebrity—I'm the Ambassadog of Hope for Animal Cancer. Here is my paw-tograph. . . .

Diagnosis. Surgery. Chemotherapy. Radiation. Rehabilitation. Just like people, animals with cancer travel this journey.

The Tails of Hope Foundation and the American College of Veterinary Internal Medicine Foundation are committed to providing education on the revolutionary care that can give companion animals a chance for a healthy future filled with hope.

If you would like information about treatment for companion animals with cancer, please contact Tails of Hope Foundation, Inc., at www.tailsofhopefoundation.org or the American College of Veterinary Internal Medicine Foundation at www.acvimfoundation.org.

I would like to thank all of the incredible doctors and medical professionals who helped add years to Jack's life—Dr. Gerald Post, Dr. Nicole Ehrhart, Dr. Jui Jui Wen, Dr. Laura E. S. Hinton, Dr. Ann E. Hohenhaus, Dr. Dawn Stelling, Dr. Claude Grosjean, Dr. Rick Altieri, Dr. George Kramer, Dr. Andrew Pepper, and Dr. Rick Rothman; Linda Blick of the Tails of Hope Foundation, Inc.; and Paula Mejia of the American College of Veterinary Internal Medicine Foundation. Special thanks to Meredith Vieira, Matt Lauer, Oprah Winfrey, Ann Curry, Al Roker, Natalie Morales, Jim Bell, Don Nash, Amy Chairo, Marc Victor, Nick Palladino, Amanda Mortimer, Fred Staab, Josh Weiner, Sabrina Clay, Joanne LaMarca, Shantel Klinger, Joan Hamburg, Jane Friedman, Linda Lambert, Deborah Trueman, Beth Remington, Barry Solomon, and Andres Romo Devivar; to all the wonderful people at HarperCollins Children's Books—Kate Jackson, Maria Modugno, Robin Klonsky, Katie Bellas, Barbara Fitzsimmons, Martha Rago, and Rachel Zegar; to my mother, Mona Rappaport, whose affection and chicken and baked potatoes made Jack howl with delight; to my sister, Linda Solomon, who adored Jack and his precious, sensitive eyes and whose beautiful photography made this book possible; to Pepe Hernandez, whose loving care for Jack sustained him; to Rick Swift for his unconditional love and support for Jack and all my "fur angels"; and in memory of my wonderful father, Daniel J. Rappaport. He shared my love of animals, and right now he and Jack are sharing a lamb chop.

—J.R.